Also by **HELEN FROST**

Keesha's House
Spinning Through the Universe

THE BRAID

HELEN FROST

FRANCES FOSTER BOOKS
Farrar, Straus and Giroux
New York

www.fsgkidsbooks.com

Library of Congress Cataloging-in-Publication Data
Frost, Helen, date.
  The braid / Helen Frost.— 1st ed.
    p. cm.
  Summary: Two Scottish sisters, living on the western island of Barra in the 1850s, relate, in alternate voices and linked narrative poems, their experiences after their family is forcibly evicted and separated, with one sister accompanying their parents and younger siblings to Cape Breton, Canada, and the other staying behind with other family on the small island of Mingulay.
  ISBN-13: 978-0-374-30962-6
  ISBN-10: 0-374-30962-0
  [1. Sisters—Fiction. 2. Family—Fiction. 3. Islands—Fiction. 4. Emigration and immigration—Fiction. 5. Mingulay (Scotland)—History—19th century—Fiction. 6. Cape Breton Island (N.S.)—History—19th century—Fiction. 7. Scotland—History— 19th century—Fiction. 8. Canada—History—1841–1867—Fiction.] I. Title.

PZ7.F9205 Bra 2006
[Fic]—dc22

                    2005040148

Dedicated with love
to my sisters
Mary, Margaret, Kathy, Barbara, Dorothy, Nancy, and Karen

Contents

Introduction

The Braid begins in 1850, near the end of the Highland Clearances, when thousands of people were evicted from the Western Isles of Scotland (also called the Outer Hebrides). The people had lived on the land for many generations, working hard and paying rent, but when it became more profitable for landlords to raise sheep on the land than to collect rent from their tenants, many landlords forced the tenants to leave. Some of the evicted tenants went to cities in mainland Scotland; others went to America, New Zealand, or Australia. Many went to Canada. They were not rich people, and often they did not have time to pack for the journey. Some left home with little more than the clothes they were wearing.

Around that time, the potato crop failed in many places, including both the Isle of Barra, in Scotland, and Cape Breton, in Canada. This caused widespread hunger among people who depended on potatoes for a large portion of their food. The effect was not so severe on the smaller island of Mingulay, to the south of Barra, in part because people there had a more varied diet, including seabirds that nested by the thousands on the island's cliffs.

THE BRAID

The Mussel Bailiff

Sarah

Isle of Barra, Scotland, 1850

All of us! Father, Mother, Jeannie, and the wee ones—Willie,
Margaret, and Flora—Grandma Peggy, and myself. We're all
to be evicted come next Monday. Our crime? Nothing more than
hunger: I went with Mother when the tide was out, to gather
mussels for our supper. We filled our basket. Mother strapped it
to her back. We could hear, from down the glen, Old Donald playing
on his pipes, a cheerful tune that Mother hummed as we walked home.
I was happy. We'd have more than seaweed in our soup that night.
Then comes the mussel bailiff, so high and mighty, like he thinks
he is the Duke himself! Him and his dogs, all snarling at us—
and he takes out his knife and cuts the straps from our basket, so
it falls from Mother's shoulders to the mud. He grinds our mussels
underfoot until the shells are just blue specks, then tells us we're
to leave our home before this week is out. Mussels in that bay,
we're told, are bait for English fishermen, not food for Scottish
children like ourselves. If they let one family take supper
from the bay, soon everyone, they say, will be taking all the
mussels they can eat. *And what,* I think, *would be so wrong with that?*
But I know better than to speak such thoughts. I hold my tongue.
A ship sits in Lochboisdale now, due to sail to Canada
next Tuesday. Father has determined we'll all make the journey,

3

and he's gone to try to sell his tools, hoping only that they'll
bring enough to pay our passage. It troubles me: how will we
build a house in Canada without them? A table. Benches.
Willie's cradle. Grandma's loom. A new bed for me and Jeannie.
I sit outside with Grandma, knitting. We're trying to be good.
Grandma frowns and clicks her needles like she's telling them
the thoughts she tries to silence. She's in no mood for talking. But
I have so many questions. The day we'll leave is coming close.
Who else can I ask? I lean on Grandma's shoulder: *How long will
the journey be? How big is the ship? Will there be dogs and cats
in Canada?* As I expect, she shushes me. She says she
has no answers. I grow silent, breathing in the smell of her
wool shawl, the smell of peat smoke and the sea, the sour smell where
Willie spat up on her shoulder after breakfast. At last she
speaks: *Child, my heart is breaking, but I'll not be going with you.
I'll take my weaving from the loom and go back to Mingulay
where I was born. My William's buried in the graveyard there, and
some days I expect that I may well be there beside him soon.*
Then she takes my head into her hands and weeps. When she sees tears
on my face, she wipes them with her fingers, soft and rough at once.
I know she wants to hold me here. I know too that she'll not try.
She gathers up her tangled wool, takes her basket back inside.

Mussels

Such beauty in the world, such strength
in all the creatures. Each mussel
somehow finds a rock to cling to,
opening when washed by water,
closing when the tide goes out. Shells
protect the living creature—blue,
black-purple, closed upon the rock,
white inside, shining like the sun.

The Braid

Jeannie
Isle of Barra

Willie fussed, and wouldn't go to sleep. It was late, we were

all packed, ready for the journey. Sarah held him tighter

than she usually does. She looked long at his face and then she

gathered him up, kissed his nose, wrapped her shawl around him, pulled

it—pulled Willie—close. She looked at Flora, then at Margaret,

playing on the floor with the wee rag doll we made for her.

Home, Sarah must have thought. *Remember this.* Later that same

night—we could not sleep—we walked together to the cove. Father

thinks that Sarah must have told me then. She did not. None of

us—not even I—knew what she was planning. Sarah was

so quiet. She didn't laugh when an otter opened a

mussel with a rock and ate it and I made my wee joke:

We'll tell the bailiff, and he'll send you to Canada. The

bay was still. Moonlight on the water made a path from our

Scottish sea to—where? Where, I wonder, will we all be eating

supper in two months' time? One year? I linked arms with Sarah,

the way we've done since we were small, sitting and watching on

that rock. Then we dipped our hands into the sea and touched our

tongues to the seawater, each of us swallowing a bit.

Canada seemed far away, the salty sea so close, our

journey not yet started. We walked back home. *Hush now,* Sarah said,

they'll be asleep. So they were, but we were wide awake when
we went to our bed. I took the hairbrush from the wooden
bench, and sat by Sarah, brushing out her long thick hair. *Oh,
Jeannie*, Sarah whispered. *I can't . . .* She drew in her breath. Then . . .
Goodnight. (Or did she say *goodbye*?) She loosened my braids, held
them in her hand, and brushed my hair so hard—I should have known.
But how could I? Then Sarah braided my hair with her own,
close and tight, so our heads were touching. We started laughing.
Will you girls go to sleep? It's near morning! Father called. Like two
cats curled together, we slept that night. Or—did Sarah sleep?
She must have stayed awake until I slept. She must have had
her sewing scissors tucked into her pocket. Sarah knew
where she was going. I woke to no warm place beside me.
She'd cut the braid close to our heads, tucked half into my hand—
You / me / sisters / always.

Now we're in the boat, and leaving;
Mingulay is but a distant blur. We've left without her—
and I want to dive into the sea and swim back home. But
soon we will be out too far to see the hills where Sarah's
tears are no doubt falling like my own. I squeeze my right hand
once, around the braid in my pocket. Father says, *Be strong.
Try to be as helpful as you can. Your mother needs you.*
Inside, I'm still crying. *I'll hold Margaret's hand,* I say.

Hair

White, shining in the sun, Grandma's
hair winds round her head, a braid, a
crown. Margaret's hair, black and fine,
damp on her cheek in fretful sleep.
Flora's and Jeannie's golden curls,
Sarah's red-brown braid—Mother's strong
hands, teasing out the tangles as
she sings into her children's ears.

After Three Days

Sarah

Isle of Barra

Were they angry? Could they understand how this place holds me, so
tight I could not live away from it? Nor could I leave Grandma.
She scolded, but she was pleased when, after three days, my hunger
pulled me back here. That first day, I hid and watched their boat go out—
Margaret kneeling at the bow, arms spread like a bird. Behind
her, Mother, strong and watchful, one hand upon her shoulder, the
same way she watched me when I was four. Flora sat straight beside
Father. Jeannie held Willie. No doubt she sang to him. Boxes
of food for the journey, and two other men—the fishing boat
was full. A man named Ranald took them to Lochboisdale. He has
a younger brother going to Canada by choice. Jeannie
joked: *He should go in place of one of us*—perhaps now she thinks
the joke has turned out true.

Grandma tells me about Mingulay:
*Our life will not be easy. We'll have fish and birds and eggs to
eat; I have no fear of starving. But winters can be long—and
Sarah, only twenty families live there. You'll be lonesome
on your own.* She looks hard at me. *I'll have you,* I say. She blinks.
*Our journey there is likely to be rough. Some say it's every
bit as daunting as the trip to Canada . . . Well, then.* We link
our arms and walk down to the cove. *Sarah's coming, too,* Grandma

9

says to Murdo Campbell, the young fisherman who's taking us.
When he sees me, arm in arm with Grandma Peggy, clutching my
wooden walking stick like it's my sister, I can't guess his thoughts.
Oh, Sarah, don't you worry, now, Grandma Peggy says. (I know,
then, I should be worried.) *If anyone can land a boat or
hold us steady in a stormy sea, it's Murdo Campbell. He's
known for landing safely on Mingulay when others can't.* My
own thoughts I keep to myself: Have I been foolish? Is this man
laughing at me? I know my hair must look odd where I cut it;
two patches on my skirt are coming loose; the past three nights I've
slept out in the hills, with little food. *Here,* Murdo says, *I
had two old waterproofs at home, and brought them both. You'd think I
knew that you were coming, Sarah.* I take the small one. He looks
me up and down as if he's weighing me, then shifts his anchor,
hands me a bailer—*just in case*—seats Grandma Peggy to his
left, me to his right, and pushes us out to sea. Grandma folds
her hands and bows her head. I look up at Murdo—his eyes calm,
but merry, arms pulling hard on the oars. He looks at me. *Aye,
Sarah, they'll be glad, on Mingulay, to have a lively lass.
Hand me that parcel, would you?* He opens it and offers me
strong tea, still hot, and a hard-boiled egg. *The birds are calling to
you,* he says, pointing overhead: gulls circling, screeching. If they
say anything, it's likely, *You, there—where do you think you're going?*

Song

The songs that enter children's ears
carried across centuries of
love, stay with them, bringing comfort,
setting their feet dancing, coming
back to them when their own children
first look up and see them smiling
or hear them weeping as they rock,
strong boats upon a stormy sea.

Going On Without Sarah

Jeannie

Crossing the Atlantic

So many people in so small a space. This ship is like
Grandma's salted herring, people packed that tight, everyone
hungry, cranky, some sick—a man died yesterday. I go
out to the windy upper deck, taking Willie, leaving
behind our crowded sleeping quarters down below. That air—
the stench of it won't leave my hair and clothes. Last night I slept
beside Margaret. She was thirsty, so I climbed over
boxes, stepped around people, to the water by the life-
boat. Even the water stinks. Father wonders if the ship
has enough water to last the crossing. He cautions me:
Jeannie, let's try not to drink too much too soon.

                                             Always, I'm
thinking about Sarah. Is she thirsty? Did she go to
Mingulay with Grandma? Or is she still hiding, frightened
to come down from the hills, but hungry where she is, alone
and cold at night? Sarah's strong and clever, and yet . . . Oh, I'm
lonesome for her. So is Mother—she bites her bottom lip and
blinks back tears whenever someone mentions Sarah. And is
everyone expecting me to take her place? I can't! I
link arms with Flora, as Sarah used to do, but it's like
Grandma trying to act like Mother. *Why did Sarah leave*

us, Jeannie? Flora asks. She's six years old—her question is
my question, too, and only Sarah has the answer. Our
thoughts of Sarah stretch from here to her like yarn unwinding.
Know this, Jeannie, Mother says, as if she fears that yarn could snap,
or trip someone—as if she can see my thoughts unravel—
*she's not lost to us. She'll always be our Sarah. But now,
my Jeannie, you'll be the oldest and we'll count on you.* (A
man walks by and looks at us. Do I look older? Or is
it my short hair he's staring at—is he laughing at me?
I glare at him—he turns away.) Though I'm the oldest *here,*
I'm not at all like Sarah! Compared to her, I'm useless.
I've never stood by Father as he works, the way Sarah
looked on, learning how to use his tools, or when to pull the
anchor when we went out fishing. *Just like a lad,* he'd say,
his eyes twinkling. As if a lad is better than a lass!

Fold these dry clothes, will you, Jeannie? Mother, usually so
calm, seems fretful. I study her. *Is something wrong?* I ask.
*Aye, Jeannie—it's Margaret. She's taken ill. The poor wee
lass was up all night. She can't keep her food down. It worries
me.* I jump up—*I'll do this later, Mother!* I go down
to Margaret, hot and sweaty, asleep in Father's lap.
They both look dreadful, and Father won't let me stay to help.
Go back up to your mother. Now! he barks. My blood goes cold.

Boats

A strong boat on a stormy sea,
blackened by tar that seals its joints,
rises on every cresting wave,
rides down again into each trough. Swell
of the water, curve of the boat,
swift mind of the oarsman who knows
the shape of each rock, each island.
Knows the way into the harbor.

Stormy Evenings, Dancing

Sarah

Mingulay, Scotland

Like a puffin returning to her nest, Grandma has come home.
Everyone here loves her, and because I'm hers, they welcome me.
Go ask your aunt if she has oil to spare, Grandma says. When I
leave, Aunt Mairi gives me a plucked kittiwake. *Something more than
air and water for your supper.* It's eighteen days now since I
slept in my bed with Jeannie. Their journey is nearly halfway
over; they'll soon be in Canada—as they move towards that
life, will they be forgetting me? Last night I dreamed about their
ship, a dark cloud above it, Jeannie all alone, crying for
me. I reached out to her, but woke before she took my hand.
I'm fretting about all of them. Grandma tells me I should try
to put it from my mind. She hands me a broom. *Sarah, why be
frightened about things you cannot know? You know your sister's not
alone.* I start to sweep. She watches me. *Nor are you,* she adds.

I have cousins here I don't know well. Aunt Mairi's sons, Angus
and James—Angus is about my age (he's just turned sixteen); James
is eight, trying hard to be as much like Angus as he can.
I go with them to the cliff top to gather seabirds' eggs. I'd
like to learn to snare the birds, but Grandma says, *No, Sarah, you
leave the birding to the boys.* I don't see why.

15

Murdo Campbell

is still here, waiting for the sea to calm. *We're lucky we made*
our landing here the day we did, he says. He sits with the men,
unwinding tangled lines, barking the nets and sails. When his line
snaps, he doesn't snap at it, as I often do if a sock
unravels while I'm knitting. I've grown used to Murdo's teasing—
now when he jokes about my hair, I tease him right back. He has
a merry laugh; I like to hear it. These stormy evenings, there
is dancing at Aunt Mairi's house, and Murdo often chooses
me to be his partner—out of kindness, I suppose. Others
here have known him longer, and are prettier by far than I.
Useless, anyway—soon the weather will clear and he will leave.

Sarah, Murdo says, *the sky is clearing. I'll be leaving in*
the morning. I carry an armload of his nets; we walk, not
saying much. At his boat, he lifts the nets from my arms. *You're a*
lass I'll not be soon forgetting. Like a lad in some ways, yet
so . . . delightful—oh, that hair! He smiles, reaches out to touch it.
(*Ask if he'll return,* I tell myself, but I do not.)
                                                    In the
wee hours of the next morning, I wake as I often do, with
worries—Mother, Father, Jeannie, Flora, Margaret—I go
down the list to Willie and find, like the braid I hold in my
lap, a new name wound in with the others: *Murdo.* I go to
help him launch his boat, but I'm too late. Already, out on the
cold and restless sea, I see his boat, him pulling hard away.

Dreams

In dreams we harbor what we know
and almost know and briefly see
between our sleep and waking. A
falling tree, a wolf track, a white
horse walking forward. A woman
wearing a white dress stands beside
an old house, smiling—*welcome*. Dreams
surface like seals, dive deep, swim far.

The Crossing

Jeannie

Quebec City, Canada

Home: it seems so far away and long ago. Mother tells

me not to think about the brutal crossing, but how can

I forget the sickness spreading through the hold, each day worse

than the day before, and nothing we could do to stop it?

I held Margaret. She shivered. She would not eat or drink.

Halfway across the sea, she died. Our sweet Margaret. And

that was only the beginning. Father and Mother spoke

their prayers, I sang a lullaby, we gave up her body

for the sea to take away. Then Flora. Father put his

hand on her hot forehead, and ordered me away. *Go now!*

Try to keep Willie warm and dry. Did Father know he might

be dying too? That night he said, *Jeannie, help your mother.*

Not gruff, as he could be—something tender in the way he

added, *There's more to you than we've yet seen.* If I'd only

known—those were Father's last words to me. That night—we had just

sixteen days of our journey left—Father and Flora both—

can it be?—died while Mother, Willie, and I slept. Now when

I try to sleep, I can't. I'm crying for them—and Sarah.

You bring me comfort, Jeannie, Mother says. I don't see how.

Why am I here? What will we do? How will Mother and I

make a home in Canada alone? Who will help us? A

man whose wife and son died on the crossing stood with us in
line as we got off the ship. Alone like us, he picked up Willie's
sock when it fell off, and then—he asked to marry Mother!
Teasing or sincere? (Mother simply said, *No, thank you*.) We
have a bit of money sewn into our skirts—but not much.
There is nothing—no one—for us here. Mother has made a
choice—we're going to Cape Breton, where we hope we might find
others from home who went there more than twenty years ago.
I wonder—will we find them? Mother was a girl when they
left—will they know her? Will they help us if they do? We get
in another line. People move away, as if we are
not good enough, or clean enough, to speak to. Willie has
a runny nose, and won't stop crying. I know how he feels,
yet I feel something else as well here—like a baby seal,
it pops its head up from the ocean of my grief, peers through
the terror of the crossing. I look around at people
with clean clothes, parcels tied with string, who know where they are
going, and I feel—hope. How is that? I have nothing but
my mother, my brother, and the ragged dress I'm wearing
to this new place, Cape Breton. Yet I have my life. I have
the one thing so many others lost. No one will take that
away. Somehow, somewhere, I will make of it what I can.

Seals

Seals dive deep, swim far, surfacing
wherever watchers don't expect
them. Look, there—a black head bobbing
in the water by that rock. Round
eyes stare at us—dark, unblinking.
Seals sing, or cry, or bark, or none
of those—that low voice all their own,
mysterious, inside the wind.

Part of the Island
Sarah
Mingulay

Tell me, Sarah, Grandma Peggy sighs, *why must you always*—I
can guess she'll say—*do everything the boys do?* She claims that I'm
worse here, away every morning with my cousins to the cliffs.
It is hard to snare the seabirds, but I'm learning. Now Grandma
drinks her tea as I tell her how I reach down from the cliff top
and slip my noose around a shag, pull it tight, catch the bird! I
speak with such excitement she does not outright forbid it. My
body aches all over. *You're so like your father,* Grandma says.
His arms could be near falling off, and he would keep on fishing.
Now she's found a pair of Grandpa William's trousers, thinking she
might take them in to fit me. *You'll be safer wearing these. Your
mother would not want you clambering around those cliffs in skirts.*
He—Grandpa William—was a large man, and Grandma Peggy can
only do so much with thread and scissors. So it is that I'm
just back from birding, dressed like an old man, guillemots in
both my hands, hair grown back a bit, but wild as the cliff-top wind—
when Murdo Campbell comes again. He laughs. My face grows hot. *Oh,
Sarah, not to worry! You're more a lass than ever. I see
how you've this island in you now,* he says. We walk to the cove.
I let the sea foam wash my feet beside a line of shells. Like
a necklace on the sand, they are: pink, blue-black, gold, some with life

inside them, one round white one, a star at its center, small as
Willie's fingernail. I hold them in my hand and recall my
mother's smile, her strength. How are the tiny shells not ground to sand?
We climb to the cliff top, raucous with kittiwakes and gulls, so
much swooping out, flying in! Murdo reaches his arm into
a puffin's burrow—we have seen the puffin fly away—and
finds an egg. He holds it out for me—most likely laid not long
ago. I take it: cream-colored, with streaks of violet-brown.
They're pointed on one end like this—he touches it—*so if they*
get too close to the cliff's edge, they won't roll off. The two of us
are standing near the cliff's edge, breakers pounding below, where they
have crashed through the arch into that sea cave forever. The egg
feels fragile in my hand—I put it in my pocket. A lone
seal bobs in the sea, dives, and comes up some distance off. It looks
through the salty haze, as if gazing straight at us. *Seals are like*
people, I say. *I know they often swim alone, but I think*
they're happier together. Murdo looks thoughtful, says, *Perhaps,*
but when you spend your life alone at sea, you grow used to it.
Wearing an old gray-blue jacket, Murdo smiles at me, and I
have trouble separating his eyes from the gray-blue sea. In
that moment, something sudden makes me turn my face away. We
can see for miles. We're both quiet as we turn to go back home.

Wind

Mysterious, inside the wind—
the seeds and sand, all the unseen
fragrances. Rain slashing down, fire
flaring up, sails billowing, clouds
forming, flying, fading. A girl's
hair whips hard around her face. Does
she hear a distant bagpipe? Or an
owl? *No, it's only me,* says Wind.

Alone Among These Giant Trees

Jeannie

Cape Breton, Nova Scotia

I see an otter sliding down a muddy riverbank.

I'm comforted a bit—one small familiar face. The sea

cliffs here are hidden behind dark forests. I remember

Grandma telling of a forest she once heard about—tree-

tops higher than houses—we thought it was a fairy tale.

I see now, such trees are real—they rise up all around us!

My eyes long to rest on a wide and empty sky. These trees

say to us: *You're small. You're nothing.*

We have found no home here.

Fishing, picking berries, we stay alive, but Mother's weak.

She still believes we may find our kin; I don't expect to.

Your kin may have gone to Australia, one man told us. Our

skirts are torn and dirty. We sleep in any shelter we

can find—an old barn when it rains, the forest when it's clear.

I see tracks of animals—large, unknown to me. I peer

into the trees and listen hard—a wolf? An owl? Or the

wind? I shiver and hold Willie tight. People stare at us—

Oh, I miss Sarah! She'd know how to make a home! But I

see no way to fetch her, and we cannot return.

A wee

cove near here is our best source of water—a flat rock is

like a table. We've learned to dig into the sand for clams.
Life sometimes feels safe on mornings when the weather's clear. Then,
as a storm comes in from the distance, I must gather all
my courage—speaking to strangers is, to me, like eating
sand, but we have to ask for shelter and a bit of food.
So we trudge along a dirt road, hungry and tired. I look
into a farmyard where a farmer tries to shoo a pig
and chickens into a pen. *Might we have an egg?* I ask.
Long and hard he stares at us—at me—my skirt crusted with
brown dirt, holes in both my shoes. He glances at his chickens—
they have all but one escaped. He looks around, then back at
us. *Where is the baby's father?* Tears spring to my eyes;
they fall before I stop them, and he holds up one precious
egg—*here*—and smiles at me. He sees that Mother and I are
alone and says, *Come with me, miss. I'll show you where you might
look for eggs.* Mother takes Willie from me then—we do not
like this man. We walk away. We both fall silent.

Do you

think . . . Mother . . . (Are there words for such a question?) *Do you think
perhaps he thought . . . that I am Willie's mother?* My cheeks burn.
It did appear that way, she answers. And then: *Oh, Jeannie,
I see great beauty coming to you.* She looks intently
into my face—is she complimenting me? Warning me?
I cannot tell. Thunder (beauty?) rumbles in the distance.
Home seems farther off than ever. I take one step. One more.

Owl

Snowy owl, silent in the wind
as evening comes on, glides past
people walking home from working
all day in the field, bringing in
the harvest. In her talons, she
too carries food, a lemming for
her owlets waiting in the nest.
She feeds them, smooths her feathers, rests.

This Secret

Sarah

Mingulay

Banking the fire before I go to bed, I listen to the
sea, the wind, a distant tune from Uncle Allan's bagpipes. I
remember a song he and Aunt Mairi sang one evening: two
trees in a churchyard, branches twined above the lovers' graves, a
tale of love that lasts beyond this life. Hearing that, I thought: *Like*
us, that love—like Murdo and myself. We'll be like those two strong
trees, roots deep, growing close together. Oh, I wish Jeannie were
here—I want to tell this secret, whisper and laugh until we're
weak (or Father shushes us). *A young man cares for me. I have*
to tell someone! Murdo whispered something to me—is this love?

Our time together was too short, three days and four short evenings.
We both hoped that—like last time he was here—the storms would not soon
clear. Grandma tried hard to keep me busy; whenever I came in, she
peered at me. Before she could ask questions, I'd go out to stack
the peat or pluck the seabirds. Evenings, at the ceilidh, she watched
us dance—I know she likes Murdo; is she a bit surprised that
I have caught his eye? All my life, it has been Jeannie—or our
wee Flora—that people fuss about. Their curly yellow hair
is prettier than mine, and Jeannie's always smiling, while I
clam up when people speak to me. Yes, I miss my sister, but

then I wonder—if she were here with me, would Murdo be like
all the rest, drawn to her, while I was lost in Jeannie's shadow?
Eating supper—a kittiwake I caught—Grandma sets down her
food and remarks about the feathers we are saving. *Sarah,*
look at these—one day, we'll have enough for a feather bed. She's
trying, in her way, to say, *When you're ready to be married—*
asking no harsh questions, but suggesting: *That will not be soon.*
(With not enough feathers for a pillow, and almost all the
seabirds away now for the winter.)

                                 Murdo is, I trust, safe
at home on Barra. I'm out here remembering his gray-blue
eyes. My family must have crossed to Canada by now—so
precious to me . . . and so far away. I am uneasy: Where
are they sleeping? Have they enough food? Has Father built a house?
Might Jeannie be as tall as Mother now? Is Willie walking?
(Not yet, I think, but likely crawling all about.) *Jeannie, do*
you have our braid? I take my half out of my pocket, and I
think of everyone I love, watching the fire's soft glow as it
burns low. Mother and Father won't know about Murdo; he and
Jeannie will not meet. I loosen the braid, spread it in my lap,
intent on picking out a sprinkling of shells—when Murdo touched
my hand, I was holding them; I dropped them in my pocket. From a
distance, no one would have known he whispered, *I'll return. We'll have*
more time together. I replied, *May you be safe until then.*

Feathers

Feathers, smoothed through fingers, rest on
a young girl's open hand: strong spines,
soft edges, nearly weightless—one
breath carries them into the air.
Above, on a gannet's wingtips,
feathers guide the flight, the sudden
plummet from a high and cloudless
sky, to the water, to the fish.

Like This Black Spider

Jeannie

Cape Breton

The days grow colder. People tell us there will soon be snow.
I don't know how we will survive. Our clothes are wearing thin.
Two nights ago we slept outside, curled close together in
a haystack; when we woke, our hair was white with frost. *Be*
like this black spider, I try to tell myself. *Find something*
strong within yourself. Climb it. Spit out more. Late last night we
were lucky to find this barn to sleep in. Now it's morning.
We hope the rain will let up so our damp clothes can dry. We
have no money left. We must find food today. All those who
love us are in Scotland—it is strangers we must ask each
evening for the simple kindness of a place to sleep.
Soon the girl will come in to milk the cow. If we're lucky,
she will give us each a cup of milk. I will offer to
stack their wood, clean out their henhouse, fetch water, or maybe
watch the baby so the mother can go about her chores.
That is how we have been getting by all summer, trading
our help for food and shelter, washing out our clothes and
hair in lakes and rivers. But when the lakes and rivers freeze?
I shudder when I think of that.

       The barn door creaks open,
but it is not the young girl I saw when we arrived. I

liked her; she seemed kind. This must be that girl's mother, with dark
shadows under her eyes. Her hands are cracked and red. *Be gone!*
(Her voice so tired—angry.) *We've not enough to feed ourselves!*
(Sarah. What would Sarah do?) *There's thousands of you starving!*
(She's kicking straw at us!) *Missy, you be careful who you
marry!* I don't know why she's shouting *that* . . . I back away.

Soon we're walking down the road again. Willie is heavy.
The sky looks clear in the distance, near the sea. Is there some
safe harbor for us somewhere? We keep walking until the
gray-blue of the sky meets the dark blue sea. It reminds me
so of home. A noisy crowd has gathered along a dock
where a ship is full of food. A man shouts out, *I have a
house full of hungry children!* The captain hears but keeps on
walking up and down the deck. He shouts, *What would you have me
do? What shall I tell my bank?* He's almost pleading with us.
I can't let them starve, says the man. The captain drops his hands.
It's as if he wants to feed us all—but how? I move up
and try to get a better look, sit down to watch. In my
lap, Willie squirms to crawl away, after a dead bird he sees. *Don't
touch!* I say. I look at the captain. He sees me watching.
A long moment passes. He turns, steps down, opens up the hold—
Have what you need, he tells us all. His crew stares open-mouthed.
Then the captain brings a bag of oats, puts it in my arms.

Food

Water from the sky and two fish
from the water. A slice of bread,
half a bucketful of berries.
So we are nourished, so we move
forward, finding in each day food
to carry us beyond that day.
From trees: red apples, purple plums.
From the ground: potatoes, carrots.

Almost Like Sisters

Sarah

Mingulay

Snow quiets us and draws us close to one another. Outside, a
thin wail of wind tries to get inside, but it does not. All our tracks,
in and out, house to house, are quickly covered. Grandma Peggy has
been ill, and today she's stayed in bed, knowing I'm here if she needs
something for her cough. She is sleeping now. Aunt Mairi has come by.
We sit by Grandma's bedside drinking tea, steam rising from our cups.
Morning stretches long. We fall into stories—almost like sisters,
we talk on. Aunt Mairi tells me that I often make her think of
who my father was at my age: *Sixteen when he left Mingulay.*
Each day that winter, he grew more restless, until he could barely
sleep. That spring—it came late that year—he went to live on Barra. How
lucky they were that Father was a fisherman, and strong. He could row home
to see them. Aunt Mairi tilts her head, studies me. What does she see?
Maybe she knows, although I seem cheerful as I go about my
chores, I ache with longing for my family. *Do you wish you could*
trade places with your sister? she asks. *No,* I answer, *this is home*
and I am glad of that. But—what I cannot say to her: Something
freezes in me when I think of them. I almost see them through an
open window—they are not happy—then the window closes, and
I feel like I am barefoot in the snow, wandering outside, some
dark place where no one knows me. The feeling passes; after it has

gone, I start to cook—potatoes, dried birds, bannocks, bread—more than we,

ourselves, can eat. I cook as if I am afraid the old times of

starving will return, and it is up to me alone to feed us.

You'll always long for Jeannie, Aunt Mairi says. *No matter how far*

away she is, you may know when something hard is happening to her.

Heavy words, to know there is something but not know what. Some deep well,

some knowledge I can't name, sends pictures to me. I take a deep breath.

The troubling part, I say, *is in what I do not see. If you ask*

me who is yet alive, and who is not, I cannot say. (A ship

docks—somewhere—in the shape of a coffin. Is this a vision or

a fretful dream?) Aunt Mairi only nods. She rests a steady hand

on my shoulder as she pours another cup of tea. It comforts

me, though she is neither Jeannie nor my mother. If Grandma hears

us talking, she doesn't show it, apart from a flutter of her

hands and a short cough when our talk takes a turn and Aunt Mairi brings

up the subject of "a certain red-haired fisherman." When she sees

my face flush, Aunt Mairi says, *Be a little careful. You're still young.*

Don't be too quick to give your heart away. I nod, but think, *Too late,*

watching what I say, in case Grandma is listening. Some dreams I

hold in a safe place. If one touch and a few sweet words from Murdo's

mouth at our farewell are all it takes to start me thinking of his

arms around me, I know enough to keep such daydreams to myself.

Potatoes

From the ground, each round potato,
russet, brown, or gold—crumbs of dirt
still clinging to its skin—just fits
into the palm of the hand that
pulled it from the earth. Brushed clean and
roasted, held again in two hands,
it offers warmth, then nourishes
the body, the hands that held it.

Looking

Jeannie

Cape Breton

A rusty saw blade, seven nails, two shells, a flat stone—large
tracks by the river make me take stock of all these things I
have gathered, in hopes that they might help us make a home here.
Need has made me bold. Mother and I built a rough shelter
by leaning branches against fallen logs, but this morning,
cups of water in the shelter are covered with ice. My
sister is not here, so it is me trying hard to think
of some way we can stay warm. When Father was a boy on
Mingulay, he helped his father build a solid stone house,
barely big enough for their family. And once he saw
how to do it, he made our own larger house. These days, that
home seems long ago, far away. Yet, in my mind, I still
see Father pick up each stone, turn it over, study it.
My bits and pieces are like those stones, and I study them.
Could I find a way to use these things I've found to make a
home for Mother, Willie, and myself? If I keep thinking,
some idea will surely come. So it is that when we pass
an old shed in the corner of a wheat field, weathered gray
and reeking of rotten potatoes, I somehow see: *our home.*
A man is whistling as he walks toward it with a torch. He
has packed dry straw around it—he means to light it on fire!

We'll clean out your shed! Don't burn it! We need a place to live!
Of course he thinks I have gone mad. He stares at us, then shoos
us off, ignores us. Are we nothing more than pesky flies?
Far across the field, I see his house. I see a woman,
her dress bright blue and white, coming toward us. Some small hope
wells up. The man lights his torch, raises it. I draw in my
breath, grab the flaming torch, and throw it on the ground. I don't
ask permission. All that has happened since we boarded the
ship comes over me—I stomp on his torch as if it's death
or hunger, as if I could extinguish them with my own
hands and feet. The woman arrives, looks at us. It's him she'll
comfort, I've no doubt, and they'll send us away. But when she
hears what I have offered, she smiles—says my plan sounds good to
her! The man shakes his head, then looks at her, at us, and nods. They
bring us a bucket, a shovel, point out a nearby stream. I
see the enormity of what we've taken on. (Two girls,
younger than myself, run by holding their noses.) We work
late into evening, shoveling the slimy mess outside.
I know it will take days. The smell will linger. But then—a
place to stay dry! For Mother to sew. For Willie to take
his first steps—most likely any day now. And what about
myself? A place to sleep and, upon waking, look ahead.

Stones

The body of the earth holds stones
of every size, spits them out
at random. A seeker somehow
finds the perfect stone, exactly
the right shape and size to fit each
space in a wall, the stones to form
each door, each window. The way each
word comes forth and finds its way home.

Around the Rocks

Sarah
Mingulay, 1851

Large storm clouds loom in the distance. Whitecaps roughen the nearer sea.
I've come with James and Angus to the cliffs. Birds are coming back—*look
here*—a pair of puffins meets after six months out at sea. They take
shelter together in their burrow. I remember Murdo, that
morning when we walked together and he gave me a puffin egg.
My eyes scan the sea—though I know it's too rough for him to come. I
think I see a gannet dive and catch a fish and eat it, rocking
on the waves. James has caught three guillemots. Now he turns toward his
house. We all decide to get back home before the storm comes. I
see Aunt Mairi rushing up here to meet her boys. No—it appears
that it's me she's looking for. *A boat is coming,* she whispers. *I
still don't know for sure who's here, but perhaps you want to come and watch.*
It doesn't take us long to hurry to the landing place. I tell
them, *In this weather, our help will be needed.* Uncle Allan takes
a rope and their pony to help pull in the boat. I crane my neck,
thinking—yes—it *is* Murdo (and someone else with him) coming in,
passing around the rocks—they should be safe now—just ahead of the
gray bank of clouds. The rain starts just as they land—he's barely made it
home before the storm. (*My home, not his. He's been gone for seven months.
He may not have been thinking about you,* I warn myself.) But this

fire in my heart is not so easy to extinguish when, in real
life, not a daydream, Murdo steps from his boat.

                                     What's wrong? Why are his
shoes more interesting than I am? He won't look my way. Everyone
flies around, pulling up the boat, chattering, laughing. (*He loves a*
woman back on Barra. He has come to tell me, so I will not
hope.) The fisherman who came with Murdo looks at me, studying
my face. *Are you Sarah MacKinnon? I'm Ranald Macintosh. I*
don't believe we've met. Does his face, too, hold something dark? Is he not
the man who took my family to their ship? (That image—someone's
death—the coffin ship.) I look away from him. And from Murdo. My
own face will show no more than his. If he does care for another,
she'll not need to hear of me. And what Aunt Mairi no doubt guesses,
she will, I trust, not tell. All these thoughts go through my mind on the way
to Uncle Allan and Aunt Mairi's house. If they see I'm quiet,
they say nothing, and when everyone goes inside, I slip away.
I go home and sit beside the fire, hold the braid, and think of two
girls laughing together when we went to sleep, or singing while we
worked. (*Where are you tonight, Jeannie? I wonder if you think of me.*)
Outside, the storm breaks over us, as Uncle Allan starts to play
a bagpipe tune, a soft strathspey. I hear in his music: *Sarah,*
take your time, then come and join us. Whatever Murdo's silence is
about, whatever news I do not wish to hear, the only way
ahead of me is out this door, through the rain, toward the others.

Puffins

How do puffins find their way home?
Like people gathered for a feast,
they fly in from the sea, return
home to their island cliffs each spring.
Nesting in deep burrows, each pair
tends one chick—see how they carry
fish in their bright beaks, head to tail,
like children in a crowded bed.

Shipbuilders

Jeannie

Cape Breton

Sea-wind here reminds me of the wind on Barra. When I go
looking for driftwood for our fire, the wind blows right through me. I
take what wood I can carry, and hope it burns long enough so
that I'll get warm before I must go out for more. We can cook
eggs and fish and bannocks on a flat stone heated on the fire.
I'm thinking about how I could make furniture: a bed, a
rocking chair, a table, or a simple bench. Willie straddles
his "horsie"—a three-foot-long log I rolled home and brought inside.
I chuckle when he whinnies like a horse, and Mother says, *It
appears that Willie is as clever as his sister.* Of course
I assume she is talking about Sarah, but I see her
watching me, thinking, and she adds, *I mean you—I don't need to
tell you that, do I?*

I've found a place, a mile away, where I
take wood from the scrap heap of a shipyard. *Jeannie, you'll break your
neck,* Mother tells me, *carrying those heavy pieces of wood
in your small arms.* But I'm stronger than she thinks. I'm happy when
the shipbuilders make errors: a curved hull, miscut—they can't use
it—and I see: a table leg. I drag it home, protect it.
Months later, I find another. If I can find one more like
this, and then a tabletop . . . but what then? If I only had

42

real tools, not just rocks to pound my bent, rusty nails. Father sold
his tools thinking he'd buy new ones here, but we've spent that money.
Everyone seems curious about our "home," but no one thinks
a young girl would have a use for a hammer and a saw. I'm
not sure I would know how to use them if I had them—I've been
studying the shipbuilding from a distance, trying to learn.
I stay hidden in the trees and watch the men haul in the logs—
not once have I seen them stumble. Each man has a job to do:
someone sets the log in place; others saw it, or strip the bark.
My favorite part is when they raise the ship's ribs, one after
another, and I first see what shape the ship will be. No one
guesses about cutting; each part is "measured twice, cut once," the
way Mother cuts cloth. The shipyard is noisy, but the men are
quiet when they're trying to fit the parts together. I go
away before they see me, and later watch them walking home
two by two, or singly, young and old. What would our life be if
we had Father here? Back home, he would almost always smile at
me when he came home, and Flora and Margaret would stop their
play and run to meet him. He'd be pleased, I think, and proud of us—
Sarah would be too—to see how well we're managing. Mother
is now sewing piecework to earn money, and I help her. One
way or another, we will soon take care of ourselves without
others helping us. Someday others will ask us for our help.

Beds

When children go to bed, the bed
becomes its own world, holding them
as they drift in and out of sleep.
The solid edges of that world
contain the softer center, hold
the blankets tight. When the child steps
out into the larger world, the
bed holds an almost weightless warmth.

You Will Want to Know

Sarah

Mingulay

Go in. I stand out in the rain, willing myself to go inside.

I open the door, look around at everyone: Murdo sitting

so still, alone—a helpless expression on his face. Grandma has

cooked some whitefish—they must have brought it in—Ranald, sitting by the

fire, looks like he wants to be anywhere other than here. He holds

a letter—can he read? Does he have news of my family? I

straddle *worrying* and *knowing*, as if they are separate rooms

inside me. But I must know. Whatever they have come to tell us,

it cannot be worse than constant worry. I sit down, and in due

course, Ranald clears his throat. Grandma sits down beside me and picks up

her knitting. Aunt Mairi, Uncle Allan, James, and Angus—we all wait

to hear what Ranald's letter holds. He looks around, breathes deep, begins.

I have a letter from my brother, Joe, who was on the ship with

your family—he writes from Quebec City. He tells of tall trees,

wood planks big enough to make houses. Oh, I'll just read it. But

when he's read about the trees, about his brother, he says, *It's no*

use. He stops. Then goes on: *"You will want to know of the MacKinnons.*

It has gone hard for them. The father and two of the wee ones—

like angels they were—perished on the crossing, of cholera. We

had no way to stop it, as it spread through the ship. Findlay had

sold his tools before he left, so Morag and the older girl had

45

money. They hoped it would get them to Cape Breton, where they seemed to think they might find kin. We hear there's hunger there. I regret that's all I'm able to tell you." The letter goes on, but I don't hear. I've been clenching Grandma's arm. *Which wee ones?* I whisper, but we see we've learned all we will learn from Ranald's letter. There's more about the giant logs—I cannot imagine them, and I do not try. What will they do—Jeannie and Mother—if they *don't* find kin to help them? A dog barks outside; the moon is full. The seals are crying on their rock. After Ranald puts his letter down, the room is quiet. One by one, the women gather round us, softly keening for my father— *the strongest, most gentle man*—and for the "angel" wee ones. Women are beside me and behind me. I close my eyes, lean into them, go, in my mind, back to the last night we were together in our home. I take the braid from my pocket, let it catch my tears. *Jeannie, if I had gone with you, could I have helped?* I know it does no good at all to think of that—and I know I'll always wonder. What were their last hours together like? What happened to their bodies? Those of us who stayed at home must go on living here without our loved ones. Mother and Jeannie—and which child? I want to know!—move on from us, one day upon another.

Now I look up at Murdo. He stands, without his jacket, looking at me gently. I see, in that same helpless look I saw before, the strength he offers. I see his love.

Letters

Holding an almost weightless warmth
(or chill) letters pass from one hand
to another, shifting borders
between the unknown and the known.
Such minute detail: a cricket
chirping by the dam at midnight;
a cracked blue plate. Someone sitting
at a table writing, absorbed in thought.

Have You Asked Permission?

Jeannie

Cape Breton

Inside my sewing basket, I've made a pocket for the braid.
Sitting by the fire, I take it out, hold it to my cheek. It
has not lost the smell of our old home, of Sarah sleeping. And
the smaller braid I made of Flora's hair and Margaret's still
holds a soft echo of their laughter, their whispers in the dark.
I've made a bench out of a rough plank and two large rocks. In the
room here beside it, I want to build a simple table for
us to sit at to eat or sew. I now have three curved legs; in
due course, I'll find a tabletop. The shipbuilders sometimes slice
up round logs, and discard any slice that has a knothole. I'm
waiting for one large enough to be a tabletop, though I'm
beginning to wonder if I'll be strong enough to roll it,
without help, all the way home, on that narrow path through the tall
trees. I know Mother won't help: *You could be accused of stealing!*
But I see them burn the scrap heap every week. I know they have
no use for the things I take. What harm can come? Mother says, *The
MacKinnons have always been honest people. We'll not be the
ones to bring shame on our family. Though no one here knows us,
we'll behave as we always have.* She searches my face, asks me,
Have you asked permission to take these scraps of wood? I say, *I
have no idea who I might ask—there are so many men there!*

To that she answers, *Then, Jeannie, you should not be going there all alone! Things can happen to young girls. These are not people I've known all my life. We're strangers here.* It makes me weary. Will we be strangers always? Those words: Things can happen. Is there a giant in the forest who will grab me? I've watched these men, and they do not seem dangerous. Mother goes on: *You've seen how a dog can lie sleeping by the fire one minute, quiet as a rock, and then something rouses it, and it's barking or growling by the door? Be careful, Jeannie. All men are not as kind as Father. I want you—and Sarah—to be strong and loving, but women must learn to be a wee bit wary. They must protect themselves.* I recall that farmer and his eggs. I think about our Sarah. I lean on Mother's shoulder—does she read my mind? *Jeannie,* she says softly, *we will pray that Sarah is safe with good people, who care for her as well as we would.* If only there were a way to know where she is and how she is. I have heard of a school where children learn to read and write, not far from here. One day perhaps Willie can go there, and write a letter from us to Sarah—if she is still on Barra, I know it would stand a chance of reaching her. Until then, I will trust that this same sea that breaks on our shores also breaks on hers, and carries love from us to her and back, somehow protecting all of us.

Table

A table absorbs written thoughts
(slight indentations in its wood),
and holds within its sturdiness
echoes of the conversations
that go on around it: laughter,
mealtime chatter, words of comfort.
It's part of all the stories, like
the constant kettle on the stove.

Such Immense Love

Sarah

Mingulay

Braided voices. Quiet conversation in the room around me.

It sounds just the same as it always has. Grandma Peggy's low voice,

and Aunt Mairi's higher one, talking calmly as they drink tea. I'm

still not certain of what happened last night—they know nothing of it.

Darkness, like a shawl around our shoulders, pulled Murdo and me close.

The birds above us in the evening sky circled home, calling out

for one another. Waves crashed onto the cliffs below us, and we—kissed.

In love, they say, as if love is a place you enter—as if we

slice open time and find a whole new island inside one moment.

I'm shaken by the strength of this. Does what we did together mean

I'm going to have a child? Why did no one warn me? I've always thought

it happened after people married—though I do remember a

tall red-haired girl who had a baby when I was ten years old. *Like*

stealing, Grandma said. It was the man she meant, not the young girl, but I

have a feeling she would think no better of me—us—if she knew.

(The girl—what became of her?) Murdo kept saying, *I'm so sorry.*

The stars came out. A white bird rose up from the cliff and flew over

us. Such immense love—even if a child is growing now inside

me, why must we be sorry for our joy? Now Murdo has gone home.

I hope you'll marry me someday, my darling Sarah. (His darling!)

There may be a child, and if there is, I will marry you. But if

there is no child now, I'll wait three years, then come back to ask you.
People may have wondered why he left so abruptly. Surely they
will wonder if he does not return! I don't know which to hope for—
a baby born to shame and scorn, but with Murdo soon beside me
and our entire life stretched out ahead, or—what would be more proper—
a courtship when I am nineteen and he is twenty-two, and then
a wedding with the hens, the dancing, and the piping. Oh, I'm
growling inside, wanting both at once, or parts of each. Murdo is
as close to me as my next thought, and I can't keep those thoughts away.
But I'm afraid. I want Mother here with me. And Father. Who will
protect me if Grandma turns against me? What woman can I ask
about such a private thing? Aunt Mairi would listen, and I've a
mind to speak to her, but I can't be sure that even she would stay
with me if she knew. She may think our whole family would be shamed.

There's something women here do for their husbands that I had never
heard about on Barra—they carry them out to their boats. Landing
here is difficult, the sea can be rough, and if the men can get
from shore to their boats with dry feet, their days at sea are easier.
Would anyone think it wrong that I carried Murdo to his boat
this morning? Now I sit by the fire, steam rising from my skirt. He
carries the braid I've held deep in my pocket for so long. Oh, keep
us, God, protect us, through the storms we both may face these coming days.

Kettle

The iron kettle on the stove
sings a low song, deep in its throat.
We pour the substance of the song
into a teacup: *Drink slowly,*
sit awhile, it croons, *remember,*
drink deep, and fill me up again.
It sends its heat into the world
while it holds one still central place.

Over the Ruts and Bumps

Jeannie

Cape Breton

Me? I ask, turning quickly to the man I have not seen, the
voice that startles me (*Miss?*) as I search through the shipyard scrap heap.
I'm sorry! I'm not stealing! You'll be burning this tomorrow.
It seems less clear now—am I stealing? The man approaches. Up
close I see he is not much older than myself. He says, *Look*
out for nails. I didn't mean to frighten you. I could nearly
kiss him, I am so relieved that he is not accusing me.
We stare at one another, neither of us speaking for a
moment. I show him the wood slice I've found, four feet across. *I*
mean to make a table, I say, then add, *I have three legs . . . I*
thought . . . His eyes widen. He glances down at *my* legs! It takes us
a minute to straighten out the conversation. Then he laughs
like we have long been friends, and I relax a bit, and smile too.
I was afraid my eyes were playing tricks on me, he says. *I*
knew someone had been round here, taking scraps. He waves away my
Sorry, I was only . . . and goes on: *All day I have been hunched*
over my work, staring at the shavings curling off the planks.
Inside my head, sometimes I see pictures. I might be walking
home and think I see a yellow cat that is not there. So—a
darling curly-headed girl, hiding in the forest's shadows?
If I am imagining you, let me know. (How would I?) *If*

you would like my help, I'm at your service. He gives a little bow.
They'll never miss this—you are right about that. I hesitate
for just a moment—he's a stranger—Mother's words come back to
me—*Be a wee bit wary*—but it's so clear that I need help.
Proper or practical—how do I decide? *Yes,* I say,
then, remembering my manners, *If you would be so kind, sir,*
I'm trying to roll this down the trail to my . . . home. He asks, *Where*
is your home? I'm John Morrison. What's your name? Could I run
away now? Must I tell him I live in a . . . potato shed?
Will he still think I am a "darling curly-headed girl"? He
asks again. I say, *I'm Jeannie,* and point down the trail.

                                               Think of

an otter, sliding down a muddy bank, always able to
stay graceful. Now picture me, slipping in the mud, sprawling and
ashamed, no one to help me up but this John Morrison, who
never set eyes on me before today. I have not only
landed flat on my back: I can't push the tabletop aside!
Get up if you can—he offers an arm. I try, shift my weight.
Easy, now. He lifts the tabletop. It rolls off, like a strong
boat on a rough sea, over the ruts and bumps. John kneels down as
he looks at my ankle, already purple and swollen. We
keep glancing down the trail, as the sky turns red, signaling the
day's end. It is at least half a mile from here to the smooth road.

Trees

Each tree holds one still central place
with its deep roots. Shelter for birds,
squirrels. Branches for climbers, fruit
in its season, and later, boards—
the sweet smell of lumber, fresh-cut,
solidity of wood-made things
(a bowl, a house, a rocking horse).
Shadows of leaves like passing thoughts.

A Long Road, Steep and Rocky

Sarah

Mingulay

The small pinching feeling deep inside me. The skirts I've piled in a
heap, so I can loosen their waists when Grandma is not watching me.
Tomorrow, I whisper to myself, *a boat will come tomorrow.*
Up in the sky, I watch the birds, soaring without shame. They do not
look to see if other birds are judging them as they build their nests.
Nearly sixteen weeks now since Murdo left, promising to come to
me if I send a parcel of feathers for him to sell for me—
a request so casual, no one would think twice about it. Now
I have the feathers packed and ready, and I wait.

                                                    Ranald is here.
I go over to Aunt Mairi's house. What news does Ranald have for
us? Everyone has gathered. I have brought my feathers. Ranald is
laughing at one of Uncle Allan's stories, but he stops laughing,
too quickly, when he sees me come in. Why? Murdo would not tell him,
(I am certain of it) what happened—yet when Ranald looks at me
my face grows hot. I take a deep breath. Effie, an old spinster, sits
hunched in a corner watching me—not unkindly. I think of those
planks in pirate stories, and have this awful feeling, like I am
walking out on one, the rolling sea beneath me. I take Effie
a cup of tea and sit beside her, losing myself in the soft
shadows at the edges of the room. I hear someone ask Ranald

if he has any news, and I think I see him close his eyes and
bow his head, as if offering up a small prayer. Or does he
hesitate to begin a story that he knows will bring us grief?

To begin, he says. *The landlords called a meeting. We heard they would*
help anyone who chose to emigrate to Canada. And they
said we'd be fined if we did not attend. So everyone was there.
"Sir" and "madame" at the start. And then they started talking about
where we would be going, and when we'd leave. At that point, two women
ran from the room, or tried to. A landlord stopped them at the door. They
shed bitter tears when they saw they could not return to their homes. Then
he—the landlord—told us that the ships were waiting. We had no choice!
Of course they had a choice, I think—didn't I run off to the hills
to avoid their ship? Anyone could do the same! Ranald goes on:
And then—men and women, old folk, babes in arms, hundreds of people
who woke that morning thought they'd be asleep in their own beds that night,
only to be on the ships come nightfall. A few of us pushed them
aside and escaped, but then they got their ropes and dogs. They threw their
weight against the ones who fought the hardest, four of them against one
strong man you know—Murdo Campbell—he was bellowing and crying
as if his heart was torn in half when they took him on that ship. Now
we all sit here in this room together, no one speaking. I feel
the whole room trying not to look at me. I see ahead a long
road, steep and rocky. I'm alone. I feel the child move within me.

Shadows

Shadows leave our thoughts concealed, hold
shimmering hands across a face
when some slight change in color or
expression would reveal too much.
They protect us from the blazing
midday sun. The comfort of the
oak tree's breezy shade, the solid
sharp-edged shadow of a building.

Outside Our Door

Jeannie

Cape Breton

A table. Willie sitting up and eating without our help.
Me—walking again, barely limping now, four months since that day.
Tomorrow, I'm invited to John's house. I'm happy, but yet
not sure of this. He says, *Mother wants to meet you*. But: eagles
nest in trees, ducks nest on the ground. Is it best for people, too,
to stick with their own kind? Mother is sewing a new dress for
me, but she's not certain either. She's seen their home, and even
now that we've fixed up this little place—we've made a sort of home
here—we'd not invite such wealthy people here.

                                                 Much has happened.
For the first few days after I fell, and John helped me home, I
was too ashamed to speak to him if he came by. Would he not
laugh at me? Thinking I could make a table. With no tools? When
he did ask questions, I could see how foolish it must seem for
me to think I could make furniture. The crude wooden bench that
sits against the wall was one thing, but how did I think I'd fit
those three curved "legs" to the tabletop, once I got it home? I
am grateful now, though, for all his help. The day he and his friend
rolled the tabletop from where it fell in the forest, laid it
softly down in the grass outside our door, John came into the
room where I sat soaking my sprained ankle. He looked all around

and said nothing about our poverty. It was weeks before
he told me his father owned the shipyard. When I spoke of the
grief we suffered on the crossing, he listened quietly. Then,
Would you like to borrow my tools to make your table, Jeannie?
They're good tools. You could learn to use them. Early the next morning,
there they were, outside our door. And he was right. I learned enough
about each one, through trial and error, to make my table.
Women can do lots of things, I'm finding, that people don't think
they can do.

        Mother finishes the dress she's sewing for me,
then has me try it on, and steps back to look. *Blue is a good*
choice for you, she says. It reminds us both of when we climbed the
hills on Barra, the color of the sky after a storm. *Put*
on the scarf that Grandma Peggy wove for you. When you meet new
people, it's good to have something familiar with you. That last
night with Sarah washes over me. I find the braids, both of
them—mine and Sarah's, and the small one I braided on the ship.
Their smell lingers, all my sisters' hair held in my hand. When my
one brother, here, says—*Don't cry. You pretty, Neannie,* I do start
crying and snuffling until Mother makes me take off my dress.
Now, Jeannie, she reminds me, *remember your manners. You may*
feel shy around these strangers, but they'll see—you're a lovely girl.
Longing for old times pushes me toward tomorrow; inside
me somewhere, a child stops crying, reaches out, and takes my hand.

Tools

With sharp-edged saws, we cut and build,
shaping what we need. A hammer,
handle worn smooth, passed from hand
to hand for generations, drives
new nails into fresh-cut wood. Spin
wool on a spinning wheel, weave cloth
on a loom. Sharpen the scissors,
cut the cloth. Needle pulls thread through.

Not Speaking, Not Crying

Sarah

Mingulay

Help me, Mother. Where are you? What would you say if you were here? All

day I have tried to hear my mother's voice. She, I know, would not heap

yet more shame upon me. *You should be ashamed of yourself.* Grandma's

eagle eye, penetrating my most private thoughts. Aunt Mairi,

too: *For shame. How could you, Sarah? Surely you knew better!* I long

for just one voice to whisper, *It will be all right.* But will it? If

even Grandma is ashamed (*Your father would be too,* she said), what

home do I have? The pony, Lair Ghlas, is also growing large. It

happened last summer; this is her first foal. She brings me some comfort.

I have moved my bed out to her byre—I lean my head against her,

not speaking, not crying, hardly even thinking, just resting here

when people are so cold. Faithful, my little dog, slept out here

for the third time last night, curled in the hay with Lair Ghlas and myself.

That takes care of the nights. Days, I walk up to the cliffs. My clothes don't

fit me anymore, so now I'm sitting in the byre, sewing.

I hear some commotion. Women approaching—there's Aunt Mairi's voice . . .

friends of hers . . . Grandma. They're all excited: *Where is Sarah? . . . Think of

it! . . . But he's never met her! . . . Mairi, she'll never be a beauty . . .*

the only chance she'll have. They lower their voices as they near me.

. . . around here somewhere. There she is. Oh, Sarah, come, we have good news!

63

Before I know what is happening, they rush me inside, plucking
the straw from my hair, fussing over my clothes. They sit me down, and
then, as Grandma gets a cloth to wipe at my face—like she did to
Jeannie and me when we were small children—Aunt Mairi explains: *This
morning we have had a visit from the lighthouse keeper.* I've heard
enough right there to understand what's going on. From our kitchen
table, I've sometimes looked across the water to the next island,
thinking what a lonely life the keeper of the light must have. But
me? Grandma speaks next: *He's heard about you, Sarah. That you are a
good girl at heart—we all know that—and . . . well, here is the good news:
The lighthouse keeper—Patrick is his name—has said he'll marry you!
Put on a clean dress and come to meet him.* I swallow hard. It is
news, I agree, but how is everyone so sure this news is good?
Last night I dreamed of Murdo holding out his arms, his eyes so clear.
Of an embrace so loving, it has stayed with me all day. Did his
ship land safely? Has he found food and shelter? Does he still carry
my braid with him, and think of me as often as I think of him?
Start thinking of your child now, Sarah, Grandma says as she smooths the
dress she's holding up for me to wear. She sees from my face that I
may not be as happy as she is. Am I now no more than a
"girl in trouble" who must marry anyone who asks me? Freezing
inside, I let them fix me up and take me to meet Patrick. His
hand. He holds it out to me. I stare at it. I cannot take it.

Cloth

The cloth through which the needle pulls
the thread is woven so tightly
it can keep out rain and sleet. Yet
look more closely—tiny spaces
allow a needle to pass through
without breaking the threads that form
the cloth. Like a solid wall with
a thousand secret open doors.

House with Two Doors

Jeannie

Cape Breton

All I want now is to be home where I can collapse in a

heap and take off this dress. How could I have been so foolish?

Grandma's scarf around my neck was small comfort when I saw that

my invitation was not what I thought it was. After my

long walk into town, I knocked on the Morrisons' front door as

if I had a right to be there—John had said, *Come by at noon.*

What made me think he was inviting me to lunch? Looking back,

it all feels so different. Even his first expressions of

comfort when I hurt my foot . . . not friendship, only kindness. *Take*

her downstairs to the kitchen, John, his mother said. *I have guests*

here. I'll be there in a few minutes. I got a quick glimpse of

"here" through the front door—a room far too fancy for someone like

myself—carved table; chairs with cushions; a table set for six.

Don't forget to introduce her to Eliza. She should be

sewing my dress in the back room. John led me to the side door.

Voices greeted him, as people looked at me—a cheerful group

of women wearing white caps and aprons. *Oh, you've brought us a*

beauty this time, John, one woman teased. Did he even look at

me when he joked back, *Don't I always, Maggie? That should be no*

news. I wonder if I looked confused. A girl about my age,

plucking chickens in the corner, said, *My sister got married*

and they need a new cleaning girl—will that be you? How was I
to answer that? Oh—I have never learned to be a stranger!
This was so new to me—a house with two doors? Servants? When John
heard the girl's question, he said to me, *When Mother comes to the*
kitchen, she will talk to you about that. She says the Western
Island girls from Scotland have always proved to be good workers,
but she wants to meet you herself. I told her I thought you'd want
a job, and she says we can use you. I just stood there. Too much
news at once—"a job" (I would be paid?); "I thought you'd want" (so, John,
you have thought about me?)—but something else—was he saying there
is someone else from home here, perhaps from Barra? *Those girls—those*
good workers? I stammered, *Who are they? Where do they live?* It was
clear he had not thought about this; he was just repeating what
his mother had told him. I looked away. I know my voice can
carry more of what I feel than I wished John to know. I told
him I could not stay. *Please tell your mother I am sorry for*
the inconvenience, I said as I backed out the door. *Goodbye.*

I may regret this later. I may wish for paying work, for
a job beyond the sewing Mother and I take in. Now this
freezing rain is soaking through my new blue dress as I walk home.
His mother. Not John himself. A cleaning girl. Not a new friend.
It is some small comfort that I never let on what I thought.

Doors

A thousand open doors closing,
a thousand closed doors opening,
so many places, all at once.
Doors slamming shut—the clarity
of that—or the soft click, goodnight,
as a busy day comes to an
end. A stranger's knock, a welcome
friend who enters without knocking.

Not the First Time

Sarah

Mingulay, 1852

A dream of Father: he comes into the byre smiling, speaks to Lair Ghlas.
Foolish pony. Did you think we would abandon you when your time came?
That foal of yours will be here any day now. When I wake up, I feel
my baby kicking hard inside me, pushing little fists against me,
as if announcing: *I am on my way.* I'm excited. Scared. Around
noon, Effie comes into the byre. *I saw you walking yesterday, out*
back of my house. She looks around the byre at the cozy nest I've made
of straw and blankets, then peers at my face, and doesn't leave. She's thinking,
taking her time. *You've cleaned the byre. Are you and Lair Ghlas expecting*
guests? My eyes fill; tears spill over. Effie wipes them away, lays the back
of her hand on my forehead. Her old hands are gentle; her gaze is deep.
Like your grandma, you are. Did you know, Sarah, I was with her when all
six of her children were born? Strong and stubborn woman. Don't worry—I'll
be with you when your baby comes. Rest a bit now, while you can. When the
door closes behind her, I am not so scared. She wasn't part of that
group that tried to make me marry Patrick. Later, Effie comes back with
a kettle of hot water, three blankets, and some clean white rags. She looks
at me, puts her hands on my stomach, nods. *Soon now. And, Sarah, there is*
no shame. It's not the first time a baby has been born to a girl your
age. And it will be some years before your child is aware you are not
married. I have been thinking the same thing. It is my secret hope that

69

I'll find Murdo, or that he might someday come back here, and not be a stranger to his child. I dream of him returning to us, building a house where we will live together. But there is no time for dreaming now. The baby is coming. Like huge sea-swells crashing through the arch on the western side of Mingulay, pain washes over me. Effie says, *It's work, Sarah—you can do hard work*. I push, rest, push. The sun goes down. I want this to be over. And then, at last— *A girl!* When I hold her, so much love comes into me, I have no words.

The door opens. It's Grandma. I search her face as she comes in, carrying puffin soup and bannocks. There's nothing I like better, and I'm hungry. Grandma says, *You can't hold those bannocks, hot soup, and a baby all at once—let me hold her.* There was a time I feared my child would not be loved, that my shame would be hers. What I had no way of knowing: Grandma, like myself, gazing at her, can see nothing but beauty and sweet goodness. *I'll tell you what I once told your mother,* Grandma whispers to her. *Whatever you need—ask me— for anything at all.* Then, to me—*Come back home now, Sarah.* I nod. *Goodbye, Lair Ghlas. When it's your time, I will come back out to be with you.* For the rest of the night, into the morning, people come by: *I made this*—a fine-woven blanket from Aunt Mairi. From James and Angus (*Welcome home!*) a feather pillow. People are kind (or curious). Aunt Mairi's friend asks, *Have you named her yet?* I answer: *She will be christened*—I have thought hard about this—*Murdina Morag. But I will call her Jeannie.*

Midwife

She enters without knocking, knows
when she is needed, knows from years
of watching, waiting, when to come.
Her hands have caught and washed and held
the newborn so many times she
knows the meaning of each breath, each
cry. As she ties the cord, she holds:
mother, child, pulsing memory.

The Working of the World
Jeannie

Cape Breton

Father would be proud of you, Mother tells me. *Of us,* I say. *We
came here with nothing. Now we have a home and enough money to
feel sure we won't starve.* Willie looks at Mother, at our money, at
me— *What's starve?* I pick him up—he's getting chubby—hug him, look
around the room. *It's when you're hungry, and you don't have food.* I go
out to my job, thinking about that. Grateful for the lunch Mother
made me, the farmer who asked, *Can you plant wheat?* I didn't know. *I
think so,* I said. He looked me over: *You're young, you're a girl, but I
expect you'll learn as quick as anyone.* It's not hard, and I walk
back home each evening with the money I have earned. It is enough.
Deep down—enough.

 And now this evening as I'm walking home, full of
all this wonder at the working of the world, planning a story
I'll tell Willie as he goes to sleep tonight, I pass the place where
the trail to the shipyard meets the road. And as I'm remembering
that day I hurt my ankle, I see John Morrison! He's walking
with a red-haired man. It's been a long time since I've seen John. He
looks pleased: *Jeannie, I was just speaking of you.* The red-haired man
is staring at me as if he's been looking for me all his life.
You're . . . I . . . Are you? Is she? He stutters, looking from me to John. *You're
not . . .* he tries again. *Would you be Sarah's sister?* And then John speaks:

72

That she is. He turns to me: *This is Murdo Campbell, from Barra,*
a fine builder. He's new at the shipyard. Then it's me stuttering:
A Barra from builder? No . . . a builder from . . . did you say—Sarah?
Now we're laughing and talking, all at once, walking down the road as
the sky splashes red and orange over us. Murdo knows Sarah!
It's true—he *has* been looking for me, and for Mother. As far as
I can tell, he knew only that we had left for Cape Breton—it's
so long ago, that journey. *Sarah went to Mingulay with her*
grandma, Murdo says. (*My* grandma, I think—I can almost taste her
bannocks!) He keeps looking at my hair, takes something from his pocket,
holds it out and shows me—the braid! Sarah's half. It is then I know
there is more to this story than I have yet heard. *I have one like*
hers, I say. *I know,* he answers, just as we reach home. Here's Mother,
her face full of questions. She recognizes Murdo. *I recall*
once when Sarah was first born, I was sick. Your mother took care of
me, and you came with her. You were so gentle with the baby. He
nods slowly, thinking hard. *I remember that . . . a little baby . . .*
you let me hold her . . . she was so small . . . that was Sarah! Holding her
made me feel strong. He stops; his face turns red. Mother holds out her hand.
Welcome—I was never able to repay your mother for her
kindness. Our home here, such as it is, is your home. Will you stay and
have some supper? I invite John, too, to be polite. *No, thank you,*
Jeannie, he replies. *I should be going. But may I come again?*

Memory

Childhood memories pulse through us,
alive in blood and in muscle,
drawn forth by words or touch, motion,
smell, color. A cool hand resting
on your forehead, pepper and salt
on scrambled eggs. A well-worn trail
from one safe place to another.
Echoes of unanswered questions.

My Questions Quiet Down

Sarah

Mingulay

*We don't want you to leave us, Sarah, but if you are certain you must go
to Canada, we'll help you.* Everyone has said this. I am looking
at the feathers Aunt Mairi has been saving for seven years. Then I
look at her, holding my baby, loving us, offering to help us
go: *The feathers are yours if you need them.*

                                  Could I find Jeannie and my
mother if I don't find Murdo? How big is Cape Breton, and how would
I begin to look for any of them? Here, I know what to expect.
I know my life, unmarried with a child, will never be easy, yet
walking these paths and hills is now a part of me. I will always have
enough food here. Grandma's house is big enough for us. And when I think
of the crossing, I shudder: What if, like Father and the wee ones, the
story of my life should end there?

                             I look at little Jeannie, knowing
where she got her sea-blue eyes, knowing those eyes will always cause me to
remember Murdo's teasing, his joyful greetings and our sad goodbyes.
Walking here, in the places Murdo and I walked together, knowing
he is far across the sea, and I have not tried to reach him? Or—a
man and a woman, searching for each other in a strange, vast land? Which
life should I choose? I go to visit Effie and ask her what to do.

You're certain he wants to marry you? The question I've not let myself
speak, out loud or silently. I'm flooded with it now: did Murdo leave
Barra more willingly than Ranald let me know? Murdo and I were
stuttering with fear the day he left here. How can I be certain his
Sarah, I will marry you was what he truly wanted? I heard it
as a declaration of his staunch love, but perhaps it only meant
Sarah, I know I must marry you. Being noble. What were his thoughts
as he crossed the sea? (No one in Canada would need to know of me.)

It's late when I leave Effie. The stars are out, Jeannie is fast asleep,
her head heavy on my shoulder. In all this, the one clear thing: I am
her mother now. One sweet strong fact amid all my questions. Deep in my
pocket, where I used to keep the braid, I keep one tiny seashell. I
know it was tossed and pounded by the sea—yet somehow it stayed whole. *Be
like that, whatever comes,* I tell myself. *Don't be crushed. Be a loving
mother—alone or with Murdo*. All my questions quiet down, and I
recall something Murdo told me about his mother. After she died
of a fever, when he was four years old, he forgot what she looked like.
He remembered only the feeling of safety that he had as a
baby and small child, when she was alive. *Even now, when I think of
her,* he told me, *I can get that feeling back*. And then he reached for my
hand, held it. He looked at me with that deep expression—remembering
her, perhaps, or reaching for that feeling he recalled. He kissed me then—
and that was the beginning of our Jeannie. *Oh, little one, I'll keep
you safe. I will try my best to find your father. If my heart breaks once
again, I will try to protect yours*. I will sleep now on this promise.

Answers

When a question seeks an answer,
the answer may run out, arms wide,
to greet it. Or it may stand off
to one side, watching and teasing
for a while, flirtatious. It may
be unsure of itself, hoping
that when the question arrives, it
earns and holds its own warm welcome.

Walking Home

Jeannie

Cape Breton

Go home! Shoo! I scold the big black-and-white dog that stands in my way looking fierce, barking at me. Walking home from working in the fields, I've been thinking about Sarah. I stop. A girl steps out, looks at us—the dog and me—growling at each other. *I've seen you out walking. My name is Elizabeth—my friends call me Lizzie. This old dog would never bite you. Come here, Duke!* He goes to her. *I see why you expect the worst, the way he barks,* she says. I've seen her too, but we've not yet met. She walks along with me, Duke trotting at her side. *How long have you lived around here?* she asks me. *Nearly a year,* I answer, thinking, *Can it be?* She's friendly—and so is Duke, when he's with her. The next thing she tells me is: she goes to school. *What's that like,* I ask, *knowing how to read and write?* She looks at me. *You could find out. Come to school with me,* she offers. I'm too surprised to answer. We say goodbye. *Think about it,* she says. *School's not hard. I'll help you catch up.* Knowing it's possible has me dreaming that someday I could send a letter to Sarah.

I think Murdo has told Mother something which she has not told me, something important about Sarah. Why do I think such a thing? What could their secret be? I keep asking myself all the questions I want to ask Sarah. Does she want to leave Mingulay and come here? If we could save money, and if there were a way to send it to her, would she come? Murdo is saving

his money to try to get back home to her. But he told Mother

it will take more than a year—she told me that much. She asked what I

mean to do with the money I am saving. I have so many

thoughts about that—a warm house before next winter; shoes for Mother,

me, and Willie; food—and now, this new dream—schoolbooks.

Just as I fall

asleep, I see—a brief flicker—Sarah, holding . . . Margaret? No . . .

Am I longing for what once was and cannot be again, or is

my mind showing me what Mother does not say? Sarah—scared, yet calm.

I think hard: What we have done this year, we can do again, if need

be. Murdo can have the money I have saved so he can go home,

love Sarah and, if I am right, their baby.

I tell Mother what

I'm thinking. She looks at me like Father did the night before he

died: *There's more to you than we've yet seen.* Only this time, Mother looks

like she can see it—this strength I begin to see in myself, too.

A long talk. We all agree: Murdo must return. Mother tells me

of their conversation. *He wants to marry Sarah, and I gave*

my blessing. I know she's young, but, Jeannie, you will have no trouble

remembering how determined she can be. If Sarah is sure,

then I am sure. Father would be pleased. I ask Murdo if I might

keep Sarah's braid tonight, so that I can weave our hair together

once again. I loosen both braids. In Sarah's I find, like a kept

promise, a tiny seashell—round, white. At its center, one small star.

Money

Warm in hands that earned it, money
lets people hold the choices they
have made, the promises they've kept.
Look at the possibilities:
possessions, generosity,
recklessness, or safety. Coins pass
from stranger to sister to friend
as clouds pass in a clear night sky.

The Brightest Star

Sarah

Mingulay

Way off in the distance, I see a boat. I've been cutting peat in the
fields all morning, with Grandma and Aunt Mairi, and we all stop to look
at the boat as it comes closer. When it passes the high cliffs, I start
walking, thinking. I've made up my mind and I'm ready to leave. Will my
dog, Faithful, think I've abandoned him? Will Grandma? Little Jeannie, will
you someday understand why we left here? The boat holds two men. We are
not certain who they are, but we know whoever comes here has had a
long day at sea. We go down to meet them.

Sarah, are you sure? I don't
answer Grandma—the feathers are packed and ready, and a parcel of
her bannocks for the journey—but no, I'm not sure. I wish she wouldn't
ask me. I'm holding Jeannie, and I stand back from the sea when the boat
comes in; I'm trying to shield her from the wind. *It's Ranald,* Aunt Mairi
says, and then she grips my elbow—*Oh! See who has come with him!* I look
up as Murdo steps ashore and strides toward me. *Sarah! I tried to
send word that I was coming, but—* He stops and stares at Jeannie. At me.
Something huge and silent holds us and surrounds us. Uncle Allan says,
*Why don't we get this boat up before we begin our telling and our
asking—it is clear there will be stories here this evening.*

When we go
to Grandma's house, Murdo sees all the feathers. *I planned to make my way*

81

there, I say, *to try to find you.* He shudders. *I'd been working and saving money for my fare home when I finally found Jeannie, your mother, and Willie in Cape Breton.* He tells how they offered to help. *I might have accepted their offer,* he says. *Some people are there for many years, trying to save money. But before I paid my fare—your mother and your sister were astounded when I told them how this all fell into place—I was asked to be on the crew of the ship we'd built. No fare to pay; in fact, they paid me to sail the ship to Scotland!* He is enjoying himself, telling this. He reaches in his pocket and calmly hands me a small pouch, golden-red-brown, explaining, though I don't need him to, *Jeannie wove the braids together into pouches. "Bring it home to Sarah," she said.* I open the pouch, and I can see at once what Jeannie has put inside—a small braid of three locks of hair: Willie's (he must have dark curls now), Margaret's, and Flora's.

          Tell us what Jeannie looks like now, Grandma says. Murdo looks at me and answers, *It won't be too long before Jeannie is the belle of all Cape Breton. But as for me—no one will ever be as lovely as my Sarah.*

          Your mother gave us her blessing, Sarah—she spoke for your father, too. Now, may I trouble those with us this evening to give permission for our marriage? Sure of myself, I stand up beside Murdo. Uncle Allan says, *I might ask what our Sarah wishes, but her smile speaks for itself. Long life together to you!*

          I have become "our Sarah" here. Murdo and I kept promises we didn't even speak out loud, that night a brighter star than we could dream of came into us, and we said *yes* together.

Travelers

When clouds part and the night sky clears,
stars are fixed points for travelers
moving away from places fixed
in their hearts as home. Going out
and returning (if they do), they
carry gifts and knowledge, pollen
from one place to another, their
part in the world's golden harvest.

Each Stalk Holds All the Sun

Jeannie

Cape Breton

The wheat is ready for the harvest. We gather it and tie it.
Look how beautiful it is—each stalk holds all the sun it's gathered,
starting with the seeds we planted in the soft, rough earth. When I raise
my head and look up to the sky, I see rain in the distance. We
will welcome it. Near the shed we've lived in, beside a small stream, we
are moving into a real house. With no potatoes buried in
a pit outside it.

Sarah received the weaving of our hair. I
don't understand all the workings of the heart, but I know something
of what her life has held since I have seen her. Even my shoulder
would not have been a comfort, had the sea not brought Murdo and his
boat back home. They sent a letter, and Lizzie read it to us. Aunt
Mairi says Sarah is a good mother—as I expected. *She
looks like you, Jeannie, with big feet and small hands,* Sarah says. They have
to ask Ranald to read and write and send their letters for them. *Tell
me, Jeannie*—Mother asks the question I have not raised out loud, she
says she's been talking to Lizzie's mother—*should you be going to
our school?* Lizzie has been telling me more about it. I want to
go, but I'm trying to save money. Willie needs shoes. If there's a
way to make or buy new beds for him and Mother, I want to try,
and it would be nice to put curtains in the windows of our house.

Your work all summer has been enough, Mother says. *I've needed your help, and you've given it without complaint. Now I'm hoping to do for you what you've done for others. You've had a long, hard journey. It's your time to be young.* I'm just sitting here, listening to this speech, all the thoughts Mother has been keeping to herself. I think back. I built this table, found a house, planted wheat. What else could I do? *If he were here,* Mother says, *Father would want everyone to have food, and after that, he would want someone in our family to read, don't you think?* (But he would not guess it would be me.) I recall when it was hard not to take the last mussel from little Flora's plate. Once we were hungry. Now we're not. Mother cuts cloth for a new dress. Willie's clothes (and all our shoes) can be mended. I will go to school.

Jeannie, have you decided? Lizzie asks. Mother nods and smiles. *I'll be right there,* I say. I go out and pat her dog, Duke, on the head. For now, I'm a schoolgirl, like Lizzie. Maybe someday I'll be a mother like Sarah, and be happy with my baby, but today I'm cheerful, walking arm in arm with my friend to school. Thinking about marriage is the farthest thing from my mind. Well—perhaps not farthest. I was happy when John Morrison stopped by our house for supper. Life may surprise me in the years to come.

                                        The tide is coming in.
I look up. A snowy owl soars in and rests on a tall tree. The brightest sun I've seen for months shines on, and in, me. As if we're all together, all our separate islands washed by the same deep sea.

Rain

Part of the world's golden harvest
is the rain the earth absorbs when
the sun disappears for days, weeks.
Soft and quiet or torrential,
falling on the fields, the lakes, fast-
moving rivers, shallow creeks—rain
moves through us, becomes visible
as beauty in the world, as strength.

We Will Be Sheltered

Sarah

Mingulay

It has never failed. The earth gives us each stone we need, when we need it.
Gathering them from the fields, we're not sure which will be of use as we
raise the walls of our home one row higher. We place one; the next appears.
We have one rule: never use the stone that's almost right. And the sea—when
we were looking for our door, something perfect from a sunken ship washed
in. (At least that's what we guess—a round glass window in a wide gray board.)
I sit outside feeding Jeannie, watching Murdo work on our new home.
Something I have noticed as I watch him set our stones: Whether he is
shouldering a big stone into place, or setting all the small ones with
his fingers, the inside wall is as well made as the outside. Sometimes
Aunt Mairi comes by, *Just to watch you smile,* she says. For our wedding gift,
she gave us all her feathers—the same ones I almost sold—so we will
have a warm bed in our new home. I'll put seashells in the windowsills,
tell my little Jeannie tales about them, and about our family.
She may never meet her namesake, but she'll be told, *Your Aunt Jeannie went
to Canada and learned to read!* Yes, Ranald has brought Jeannie's letter
to me—full of news, and: *We have seals in a bay nearby. We have found
a place to gather mussels. I've even seen puffins on Cape Breton.
Try not to forget me, Sarah. My love, Jeannie.* She knows I won't! Our
houses may be too far for us to travel, but I will remember.

Your house will soon be ready for a roof, and it's good thatching weather.
Do you want help with that? Uncle Allan asks. *Yes,* we answer, *let's try.*
It's not so hard, with the right tools and enough help. And so, with little
speech but much care, much laughter, our house is finished with a golden roof.
I tuck Jeannie into Murdo's arms, kiss them both, and we go inside.
If winter winds blow in off the sea, they'll howl outside, but we will have
food in our home, we'll have one another—we will be sheltered. Grandma
reads the sky, comes to tell us a storm is on the way. *It may pass by*
when we're asleep, she says, *but there's no question we will feel it. Here's a*
plate of fish for the first meal in your home. It's a long time since Grandma
dressed me in Grandpa William's trousers and let me go to the only
school I cared about: the cliffs, the birds, the wild sea. She smiles now, and says,
I dreamed of my grandmother last night. She had a way of tilting her
head like you do, singing that song to Jeannie. I put peat on the fire.
A kettle boils for our tea. The storm breaks on our roof. We're warm inside.

Today when I cleaned out the byre, I looked at Lair Ghlas with her foal, thought
about the morning Effie asked me to help her be the midwife. The
farthest I could see that day was afternoon. Then evening came; we ate
supper in the byre, waiting with Lair Ghlas as shadows gathered round us.
In the morning, there they both were—Lair Ghlas with her new foal beside her,
the soft light of the byre bathing them. Effie had gone home, so I was
all alone with them, holding that quiet moment in my mind. Like the
sea, it washed ashore, went out, leaving a braid of seashells on the sand.

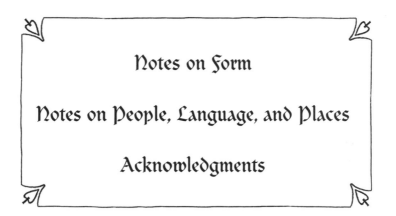

Notes on Form

I invented a formal structure for this book, derived in part from my admiration of Celtic knots. The structure has three elements:

- Narrative poems, in two alternating voices.
- Praise poems, each of which praises something named in the narrative poems.
- Line lengths based on syllabic counts.

The Braid

The praise poems are braided horizontally. The last line of one praise poem is braided into the first line of the next praise poem. The last line of the last praise poem and the first line of the first one are braided together.

The long narrative poems are braided vertically. The last words of each line in one narrative poem are the first words of each line in the following narrative poem, sometimes in a slightly different form. Where a line is broken into two parts on the page, only the last word of the last part is braided. Where the last word of a line of one poem has no context in the other story, another word in the line is used as the braided word in the following poem.

At the end of the story, Jeannie makes a weaving of the braid, and this is reflected in the form. Images and words from the first two narrative poems, as well as the subjects of all the praise poems, are woven into the lines of the last two narrative poems.

Syllables

In the narrative poems, the lines all contain the number of syllables of the age of the speaker. At the beginning of the story, Jeannie is fourteen, and the lines in her poems are fourteen syllables each; Sarah is fifteen, and her poems are composed of fifteen-syllable lines. By the end of the story, Jeannie is sixteen and Sarah is seventeen, and the lines of their poems are correspondingly longer.

The praise poems are all eight-line poems, with eight syllables in each line.

Notes on People, Language, and Places

People

All of my characters are fictional. I have chosen names that might have been used in the time and place of my story, and many of those names are still common in those places today, but any resemblance between my characters and real people, living now or in the past, is unintended.

Language

The characters in this story would have spoken Gaelic, a language still spoken in many parts of Scotland and Nova Scotia (especially on Cape Breton). The only Gaelic I've used is the name of the pony, Lair Ghlas, which translates as "gray mare."

Most people in that time and place could not read or write.

A few terms will be unfamiliar to contemporary readers. Most can be understood through the context, but two may need further explanation: The "mussel bailiff" was the one whose job it was to see that people did not gather mussels without permission. (Mussels are a kind of edible shellfish that were used as bait in the fishing industry.) "Barking the nets and sails" refers to a procedure used in tanning nets and sails to keep them from rotting. People boiled bark from oak trees and soaked the nets and sails in the solution. (The bark was imported, probably from Spain, as oak trees did not grow on Barra or Mingulay.)

Places

Cape Breton is an island on the eastern end of Nova Scotia, one of the eastern maritime provinces of Canada. Cape Breton's culture is rich and varied, with influences from many parts of the world. The Scottish/Gaelic influence is an important part of it.

Barra is an island off the west coast of Scotland. The islands of Lewis, Harris, North Uist, Benbecula, South Uist, and Barra, along with numerous smaller islands, comprise the Western Isles, also known as the Outer Hebrides. They are rugged and beautiful, rich in cultural heritage and natural life. Many seabirds nest in their cliffs.

Mingulay is a small island to the south of Barra. People lived there until 1912. In 1977, when I was teaching in Scotland, I spent a summer camping on Barra, and I was given permission to go to Mingulay for one week. The wild beauty of its cliffs and coves and seashells, the mystery of its empty houses, and the sounds of the wind, the sea, and the seabirds have nourished my spirit ever since.

Acknowledgments

I thank Frances Foster for her insights and gentle encouragement, and everyone at FSG for all they do.

I am grateful to the Indiana Arts Commission and the National Endowment for the Arts for supporting my research trip to Scotland, and to the many people who helped me on that trip, and on a trip to Nova Scotia. I name them here, and thank them for their knowledge and generosity, though most of them did not read the book before publication and bear no responsibility for any errors.

Thank you, Lena Callaghan; D. D. and Peggy Campbell; Sandy and Morag Carmichael; Anne Garvin; Mark and Maggie Hudson; Mary Huige; Andrew Kerr; Collette and Robin Mackie; Linda MacKinnon; Mairi Ceit MacKinnon; Catherine MacLean; Donald MacLeod; Anne and Ranald MacNeil; Iain MacNeil; Joe and Mary Macneil; Morag MacNeil; Rhoda MacNeil; Teresa MacNeil; John Pendrey; Solveig, Richard, and Tara Taylor; Sr. Marie Tighe; and Carol and John Walker.

I'm grateful for the friendship of many careful and honest readers, and for a two-week residency at the Anderson Center at Tower View, in Red Wing, Minnesota.

Jay Underwood, president of the Nova Scotia Railway Heritage Society; the Gaelic College in St. Ann's, Cape Breton; Dualchas Heritage and Cultural Center, in Castlebay, Barra; and the Allen County Public Library in Fort Wayne, Indiana, were all helpful in tracking down information. Of the hundreds of sources of information I used, one was especially helpful: Ben Buxton's book *Mingulay: An Island and Its People* (Birlinn Ltd., 1995).

I thank my large extended family and especially my husband, Chad Thompson, and our children, Lloyd and Glen. The bagpipes you hear throughout the book are Chad's.